How to Make Profit in Share Market

AF527537

How to Make Profit in Share Market

Mahesh Chandra Kaushik

PRABHAT PRAKASHAN

No part of this publication can be reproduced, stored in a retrieval system or transmitted in any form or by any means, electronic, mechanical, photocopying, recording or otherwise without the prior permission of the author and the publisher.

Published by
PRABHAT PRAKASHAN PVT. LTD.
4/19 Asaf Ali Road,
New Delhi-110 002 (INDIA)
e-mail: prabhatbooks@gmail.com

ISBN 978-93-5322-308-3
HOW TO MAKE PROFIT IN SHARE MARKET
by Shri Mahesh Chandra Kaushik

Edition
2024

© Reserved

Price
₹ 300.00 (Rupees Three Hundred only)

Printed at
Narula Printers, Delhi

Shri Shri 1008 Satynarayanji Falahari Baba is my Guru (the spiritual teacher).

Respected Shri Maniram Setia, retd. principal, who guided me in my childhood, helped me imbibe moral principles and taught me that 'Work is Workship'.

Foreword

This book is an excellent work by Mahesh Kaushik. This book focuses on small retail investors and gives them splendid ideas about investment. The author of this book uses very simple language and avoids technical words, making this book very easy to understand and interesting to read. Every stock market beginner must buy and read this book because it will answer all his questions about the stock market.

After reading this book, you will understand why some people always make money from the stock market and why others are always losing money in stocks.

This book can change your vision about the stock market, and I do not doubt that if anyone follows Mahesh Kaushik's theory strictly with discipline, then his initial investment of $100 will grow to $7,18,03,722 after 20 years as the author of this book claims in Chapter 2.

So I am clearly recommending 'How to Make Profit in Share Market' as an essential need of every investor.

—Dr. Ramswarup Pareek
M.Sc., M.A. (Economics), Ph.D.
Lecturer in Economics
Resource Person of Securities and
Exchange Board of India (SEBI)

Preface

I am a government servant but always wanted to build my own business. When I heard about stock market trading, I found it to be the world's simplest and smartest business because we can start this business with a minimum amount of investment and no space is required for this smart business.

In stock market investing, there is no need to invest a lot of time; you can manage your stock market business on a part-time basis. I started my stock market investment in 2005. I called it my retail store of stocks. In this retail store style, my portfolio looks like a retail store where some small quantity of most of the valuable stocks are available for sale; read the first chapter of this book for detail. When I entered the market, my friends said that 'the stock market is very dangerous for a small investor like me'. They thought I would lose my investment in the market, and I would go bankrupt. My friends are right because most of the small investors don't treat their stock market investment as a business; they treat it as speculation and want to make some easy money. But I always treat my stock market investments as a business, and as a retail shop. I am winning in the stock market and always make money from it.

In my earlier years of investing, I was not a specialist in the stock market. I was a small investor like you and developed my theory of winning in the stock market. Now I have passed

NISM certification for research analysts and have become a SEBI registered research analyst.

I have shared my 12 years of stock market winning experience in my blog at www.maheshkaushik.com over the last seven years.

In 2013, I wrote this book to help small investors. If you read this book step by step and follow the ideas given here, then you will never lose in the stock market. After reading this book, you will learn how an initial investment in the stock market of $100 will grow to $ 7,18,03,722 in 20 years.

So enjoy investing in the stock market and send me your comments and suggestions about this book and any questions about my theory. I will be glad to reply your e-mails.

My special thanks to:

1. Shri Shri 1008 Satynarayanji Falahari Baba, who is my Guru (the spiritual teacher).
2. Respected Shri Maniram Setia, retired Principal, who guided me in my childhood and moulded my moral principles and taught me that work is worship.

—Mahesh Chander Kaushik
TRA Pindwara Dist. Sirohi
Rajasthan
e-mail: mahesh2073@yahoo.com

Contents

1
Treat Your Stock Market Investment Like Any Retail Business

Most of the retail investors (small investors) invest all of their money in a single stock, or some of the small investors invest all of their savings in 12-15 popular stocks. If unfortunately, these stocks underperform in the market, then their portfolio value will be down 40-60% within a short period. Then these small investors blame their luck and criticise stock market investing.

I think this strategy is not a good investment strategy. So I invented a basic idea of best investment strategy like a retail shop. Why don't retail investors treat their stock market investment like a retail shop? I think they want to make easy money from the stock market, and they want to become millionaires in a short period with the help of the stock market. However, they are going about it the wrong way! The stock market is not an easy money making tool. If you use stock market investing incorrectly, then you will lose your money, but I will give you an idea about how to become a millionaire with the help of diversification and patience.

In my stock trading strategy, I treat myself as a shopkeeper of stocks. I invest only Rs. 6400 in a single stock. The question that immediately crops up in your mind is, 'what is the logic behind Rs. 6400, why is it not Rs. 5000 or Rs. 10,000 or any other amount'? Please do not worry. I am going to clear everything here. I put my basic investment amount in every stock, but this amount is not a fixed amount. In 2005, when I bought my first stock, I fixed Rs. 2,700 as the basic amount of every stock and increased this basic amount every year by 7.5% increment, so for the year 2017, the basic amount was Rs. 6,400. I give more details of this point in Chapter 13 of this book. Please read the full book and do not skip any page because every page is necessary for your stock market journey with me.

My portfolio is like a retail store where many varieties of dividend-paying stocks are available for sale. I never use stop loss or never worry if a stock traded below my buying price because I know that I buy a good fundamental dividend paying stock, and one day I will sell my stock with 15% + profit. If my stock doesn't achieve its target, I enjoy dividends in my holding period.

Example of shopkeeper Dalip Bhai Mali: About ten years ago, I went to a general store and asked some questions. Shopkeeper Dalip Bhai Mali's answers touched my heart. They helped me to design my trading policy, and I found that investing in the stock market like a retail shopkeeper is a very successful policy. The first question I asked him: 'In your retail shop, do you have some items which are not in demand and the items not sold in the last 2-3 years'? He replied, 'Sir, I have many items which have not been sold for the last three years'. (Then why worry if our stock is not selling in 2-3 months?) I asked him 'Are you ready to take a loss on these items, if I offer you half prices'? He replied 'No Sir, I sell these items only at a profit because one day demand for these items may occur again. It happened so many times in the past, and if I take the loss of these types of items, then I will never make profits'. (Remember, his store item does not give him dividends, and my stock gives me dividends because I always buy dividend-paying strong companies stock). My third question to him: 'Are you ready to buy more quantity of those items that are not selling well'? (In stock market language, the average out of the stocks when they fall). He replied 'No' and looked at me like I am the biggest fool in the world. Now I asked him, 'What profit do you make on each item'? He replied, 'Nearly 15% on each item that I sell'. (Then why are we greedy about our stock returns?) I asked again 'Do you feel an emotional attachment to any profit-making item and think this is like gold, so you don't want to sell it at any price because you think it will make you a millionaire if you hold it for a long time'? The shopkeeper looked at me strangely, and in reply, he said, 'Sir I think you are not sleeping well, and you may require a visit to your psychiatrist soon because no shopkeeper in the whole world feels an emotional attachment to any item in his shop'. I laughed and felt sorry for asking such foolish questions and disclosed to him that I just wanted to compare my stock market business to his retail shop business. I saw some cooking spices like red chillies, coriander, etc. in his shop, and asked him 'When did you buy these spices from your supplier'? He replied, 'I bought these spices from the broker when the price of each particular spice was down due to the new crop, so every year the market gives me a chance when I can buy spices at a low price and sell them at 15-30% profit for the whole year'. I think 'A retail shopkeeper understands the market because he would never put all of his money in 1-10 items. He never put stop losses in good quality items, he never averages out a non-performing item, and he always adopts a buy at low and sell at high theory, he sells an item for more than 15% return and rotates his money; he is not greedy with any item'.

Then I adopted this policy and found it is the best

policy for a retail investor. So I recommend that you invest only a small amount of your money in a particular stock. I recommend diversifying your portfolio, if you have more money then try to diversify your portfolio even more because the stock market has so many good listed companies. If you are a beginner who is just starting his stock market investing, then, first of all, divide your investment amount into small lots, for example, invest only 10% of your monthly income in each company stock. It means to fix your basic amount for every stock and 10% of your monthly income is a key indicator of this basic amount. For example, if your monthly income is Rs. 27,000, then fix 10% of this amount 'Rs. 2700' as your basic investment amount for every stock. So, if your monthly income is Rs. 27,000 and you want to invest Rs. 50,000 in the stock market, then instead of investing all of your money in a single stock, invest Rs. 2700 in 16 companies. (Rs. 2700 × 16 = Rs. 48,600; hold the remaining Rs. 1,400 in cash and every year save 10% of your monthly income to increase your investment. I will clear this point in the next chapter).

❒

2

The Power of Shopkeeper Approach

If you hold 200 quality stocks which you buy at different lower levels, then it is not difficult to sell two stocks per day at 15% profit. Suppose, all of your stocks are in $100 lots, then if you sell only two stocks per day, your profit is $15 per lot and this means your daily earning is $30 per day or $900 per month. And when you have 2,000 stocks in your retail shop, then you will be able to book 15% profits per day in 20 lots, meaning your daily earnings will be $300. The example given here is not a guaranteed income. The results may be varied depending on your buying price and market conditions. With the help of these examples, I want to teach you the power of patience and diversification. When you sell a stock, reinvest your principal amount in a good quality stock which traded at a lower price. In the forthcoming chapters of this book, I will tell you more about how to identify a good quality stock at a lower price.

Summary

1. Never put all of your money in a single stock, instead choose 2-10 stocks. And try to diversify your portfolio like a retail shop with more stocks.
2. Always buy a good dividend paying stock in the market; but when it is traded at a low price.
3. Never average out a non-performing stock. Forget about it for now and wait for the company to improve.

4. Do not be greedy. When a stock gives you 15% + return, then sell it and rotate your money.
5. Always start your buying with a low priced stock of a promising company.
6. Decide on a minimum investment amount for a particular stock, for example, if you have $50,000, then you will be using $100 for investing in each company and buy stocks from 500 good dividend paying companies, based on your research.
7. Do not buy stocks from more than one company in a trading week, because that will give you time to research the fundamentals of companies and give you the chance to buy the stock at a lower price.
8. Remember that investing in the stock market should be treated as an active business. You need to spend 1-2 hours of your time every day for researching which companies are paying dividends and find out current stock options from fundamentally sound companies, which are available for a low price.
9. Build your stock market retail shop with the power of patience and diversification.

'A retail shopkeeper understands the market because he would never put all of his money in 1-10 items. He would never put a stop-loss in good quality items. He never averages out a non-performing item, and he always adopts a buy low and sell high theory, he sells an item for more than 15% return and rotates his money; he is not greedy with a single item like the average consumer'.

❐

3

How to Make $7,18,03,722 with a $100 Initial Investment in the Stock Market

In Chapter 1 of this book, I told you about the power of the shopkeeper approach. This shopkeeper approach may be summarised in these words:

'If you have 200 quality stocks which you buy at different lower levels, then it is not difficult to sell two stocks per day at 15% profit. Suppose all of your stocks are in $100 lots. If you sell only two stocks per day, then your profit is $15 per lot which means that your daily earning is $30 per day or $900 per month. When you have 2000 stocks in your retail shop, then you will be able to book 15% profit per day in 20 lots, meaning your daily earnings will be $300'.

In this chapter, I will explain another idea in which if you have only $100 in stock market investing, then how you can start your stock market business. How is that possible? Let's find out. Divide your $100 into four parts of $25 each. Buy one good dividend paying low price stock per month with your $25 (when you read the other chapters of this book, you will automatically learn how to identify a good dividend paying stock at a low price). Also, add $10 per month to your saving account to increase your stock market investing. (If you read the first chapter, you remember I suggested that you add

10% of your monthly income to increase your stock market investment). This $10 additional saving per month will add $30 to your investment amount. This additional $30 saving will enable you to buy one extra stock in every three months.

I believe, within three months of buying, it is not hard to sell a good stock with 15% profit. If you reinvest your 15% profit and rotate your money every three months with 15% profit, then your annualised profit of 1 year is 74%. Consider an extra 10% as dividend gain, so net annualised return with the dividend is 84%. If you initially invest $100 and add $10 per month and your money is growing 84% annually, then after 20 years, you have nearly $7,18,03,722.

The first edition of this book was published in 2013. One reader of this earlier edition did not agree with the idea, so he put this negative review on Amazon site:

'If you don't know about stock market please don't write or at least mislead people. You are talking about 15% profit for every share, are you joking with people. Worst book I have ever read. If I can complain to Amazon about your misleading book, I will surely write about this useless book'. So in this edition of my book, I want to add my reply to this review, 'The example given here is not a guaranteed income. Results may vary based on your buying price and market conditions, but if you follow all of this book concept before buying a stock, then you get average 15% returns in a quarter'.

If you still do not believe in this theory, then please visit my Sharegenius blog, where I write a complete step by step story with practical examples that how a notional girl (Chinki) earned Rs. 4,73,90,45,652 ($7,18,03,722) from an initial investment of Rs. 6600 ($100). I provide you with the link to this story:

http://sharegenius.maheshkaushik.com/2016/10/

how-chinki-earn-inr-4739045652-from.html. If you buy the paperback edition of this book and feel it difficult to type the above link, then simply Google 'How Chinki Earn' and you will find above article link. Let's repeat this idea in simple words: Your initial investment is $100, and you book 15% profits every three months and reinvest the profit back into the market. With this method, you can easily get a 74% return in a year. Add 10% as dividend amount. So your net annual return is 84%. Save an additional $10 every month to increase your portfolio. One of my followers complains that it is not possible that we get profits in every stock. I agree that stock market is uncertain and it is not possible that we get profits in every stock, but if you read this whole book without skipping any page and follow my concepts before buying any stock, then we get profits in nearly 80-90% of our buying. Visit my website www.maheshkaushik.com and check my earlier recommendations. You will find that 80-90% of my recommendations got 15-300% or even more profits. So if you book 15-300% profits in 80% of your buying and book some loss in 20% of your buying, then your net profit is still above 15%. So I request that you please be patient and before giving any negative review, read the whole book and check my website. I am sure that if you understand my whole theory, then you will never criticise this theory and use the stock market as your 'Cash Cow'.

Summary

1. When you sell a stock, reinvest your principal amount in another good quality stock.
2. If you sell a stock with 15% profits within three months of buying and reinvest your 15% profit plus rotate your money every three months with 15% profit, then your annualised profit for one year is 74%.

Also, consider 10% additional as dividend income, so your net annualised return with dividend is 84%.

3. If you initially invest $100 and add $10 per month and your money is growing 84% annually, then after 20 years, you have nearly $7,18,03,722.
4. When your trade gives you 15% of profits, then hold it with a trailing stop-loss, 15% is the minimum range of profits, but it does not mean that you sell your stocks at a trigger price of 15%. After 15% gain, watch your stock closely.

❐

4
Innovation of the Base Price System

I have worked in the stock market since 2005; I know that stocks are volatile. In the stock market, no one can say what the right price to buy a stock is, or when it is the right time to start selling stock. I checked and learned about various technical stock analysis methods like technical, 200 DMA, and fundamental analysis, but no one is successful more than 50-70% of the time. So my research was not complete with the old criteria like P/E, EPS, Book Value, DMA, ROCE, etc.

Finally, I found a new term: base price (3 years' average price) and I think this may completely change your thinking and you will always like to check the base price before investing in stocks.

Base Price

Suppose, you want to buy an average feature android mobile phone. The basic price of an average feature mobile phone is near Rs. 10,000, but you have no idea about its basic price, and the shopkeepers demand Rs. 50,000 price for this android mobile. If you have no idea about basic price and the shopkeeper sells his phone at five times higher price, then what happens? The same theory is useful for buying in the stock market which means that before you buy a stock, it is necessary you have a basic idea of the stock's last 3-year average market price. So the base price of a stock is an average price of the last three years trading session's closing price.

Base price shows the real fair value price of stock according to the market. In other words, we say the base price, means three years' DMA of stock. In the calculation of the base price do not forget to adjust for bonus and stock split. For example, if a Rs. 10 face value stock market price is Rs. 100 and the stock splits in Rs. 2 face value, then you would count before the split price as Rs. 20 instead of Rs. 100. Remember for the base price or 3 years' DMA calculation, your stock must be listed for three years because if you calculate the base price below three years' price, then the calculation does not work properly.

Why Use Base Price?

Suppose you want to buy a 165-litre fridge, and you go to the shop, salesman shows you models, and you choose one good model for yourself. Now you ask about the price, and the shopkeeper says 'Sir, the price of this fridge is only Rs. 60,000'.

What happens?

Why do you think the price of Rs. 60,000 is not genuine for the 165-litre fridge?

You think so because you know that the base price of that fridge in the Indian market is nearer to Rs. 10,000-14,000 and Rs. 60,000 is an unfair price. Same would happen in the stock market if you knew base price of stock, then you have a lumpsum idea about the fair value of the stock, and you can easily identify overvalued stocks.

How to use base price or 3 years' DMA in stock selection for investment

If a stock has crossed its base price in upside and traded 10-20% higher than the base price, then I think the buying price is a good value, but on the other hand, if the stock crosses its base price from upperside to downside, then that stock is risky to buy. If you buy a stock below the base price, then it is cheap but your waiting period may be 1-2 years for a decent return and if your stock market price is more than 20% of the base price, then the valuation of the stock is already high. My simple formula for investment horizons is to buy below 20% of the base price and sell above 20% of the base price. But for trading purposes, buy 5% above the base price in an uptrend (uptrend means the stock crosses its base price from lower price to upper price) and sell 15% above the base price.

How to calculate Base Price or 3 years' DMA

Base price for three years' moving average is a new concept to me, so no software is available to calculate it. We calculate it manually with the help of an MS Excel spreadsheet. For calculating the base price, we download the last three years' closing prices of a particular stock from an exchange website and when the sum of the last three years' closing price is divided by the number of trading days, we get the three years' average price. You may also watch my YouTube video to learn how to calculate base price, here is the link:

https://www.youtube.com/watch?v=qR6EQk1f1cM or search 'Mahesh Kaushik base price' on YouTube. For example, we choose a stock NOCIL. The base price of NOCIL is 20.52 (on 12 April 2012), so CMP 16.50 of NOCIL is a fair price for an investment of 6-24 months' horizon and the target is 24 + to book profit. But for trading, I wouldn't buy it at CMP and wait for it to cross 21 and after crossing 21, I would buy it for trading purposes and book profit near 23-25 in the short-term; in trading, base price also works to stop-loss.

New Update in New Edition of this Book: One of my followers who brought an earlier edition of this book asked me a question about its base price confusion. I include this question and my answer in this new edition to improve the reader's understanding of this concept.

My follower wrote

'I have some queries about base price after reading your book'.

In Chapter 3

1. If base price is less than 20% CMP, then buy. I understand it makes sense.
2. If base price is more than 20% CMP, then don't buy. I understand it makes sense.
3. But as in the book, if the base price is more than 20%, how can we consider in point two and three whether it is 'don't buy' or 'Value Buy'?

Also, how to predict the best price when to buy after seeing all the fundamentals according to book?

My Reply: Please read this full quote in the book 'If a stock just crosses its base price in upside and traded 10-20% higher from the base price, then I think buying price is a value buy but in the opposite case, if the stock crosses its base price in downside, then it is risky to buy'. It means if the stock price is up from its lower price to higher price and traded 10% above base price but still doesn't cross 20% upside from base price, then it is a value buy. If it crosses more than 20% upside from the base price, then I would not buy it because I think the valuation of this stock is already higher from the base price.

Summary

1. Always buy a stock below 20% of its three years' average price (which I called base price) and try to book profits above 20% of the base price.
2. For calculating base price, use historical price data from companies and an MS Excel sheet.
3. Traders may use base price as a stop-loss.
4. If a stock has just crossed its base price in upside and traded 10-20% higher from the base price, then

I think the buying price is a value buy, but in the opposite situation if a stock crosses his base price in the downside, then it is risky to buy.

❐

5

Net Sale Per Share Concept for Fundamental Target Price of Any Stock

In the last chapter, you learnt that before you buy a stock, you must check 'base price' of that stock and buy only if the stock traded '20% lower than the added 20% of the base price'. If you check the base price before buying, this will automatically protect you from overvalued stocks. Now the next important thing which you must check before buying is 'Net Sale Per Share'. In the stock market, many of the average investors use EPS and P/E concepts for checking any stock valuation. But I am not satisfied with these old criteria for evaluating a stock. (EPS means earnings per share when we divide net profit by total number of shares, we get EPS, and P/E means price/earnings; this is a ratio of stock market price and EPS). If we check EPS and P/E, then we consider only profit-making companies because EPS calculated on the net profit basis and profit-making companies always traded at a high valuation. So it is wise to invest in a loss-making but good fundamental company which can turnaround in profit. Suppose, a good company X has a decent net sale of 100 million dollars, but due to company expansion plans (investment in new branches and stores), the company shows an expenditure of $ 120 million. So you see a net loss of $ 20 million and EPS or P/E is zero (or in minus sign). On the other side, a fraudulent company Y has net sales of only 20 million, but the company shows extraordinary income from selling off assets of 55 million and expenditure of 10 million. Then this company shows a net profit of 65 million (20 net sales + 55 extraordinary incomes = 75 – 10 million expenditure = net profit of 65 million). So which company is good in –X on Y? X is good because after the period of company expansion plans, company expenditure will be reduced, and the company will make a turnaround from loss to profit.

So if you use the net sales per share ratio, then it is quite an interesting thing, and you may be picking a good loss-making company at a lower valuation with the possibility of turning around. For analysis of this method, take the last quarter of the net sale figure (net income or net revenue) of your company and divide it by the total number of shares, this ratio is called net sale per share for a quarter.

Multiply this Net Sale (Net Revenue) Per Share for a Quarter by four, then this is our estimated net sale per year.

You may also calculate directly last year net sale per year (NSPY). Take last year's net sale figure, divide it by the total number of shares, and you get last year's net sale per year.

I also call it 'Valuation Meter of a Stock Price'. 'If your stock price is lower than NSPY, then your stock valuation is good, and if CMP is higher than NSPY, then the stock is traded at a higher value'. For example, for June 12 quarter, net sales of Arvind Ltd. is 852,07,00,000, and total number of shares are 25,80,43,069, so when we divide net sale/total number of shares, we get a fraction 33.02, now we multiply this 33.02 by 4 and get 132.08. So one year estimated net sale per share is 132.08, and this is a fair valuation for Arvind Ltd; as per this theory, CMP of 71 is cheap for buying and the fundamental target price of Arvind Ltd. is 132+.

Please remember if sales increase year by year, then

NSPS also increases. This book's first edition was published in 2013, so above example represents 2012 net sale per share of Arvind Ltd. If we recalculate 2017 net sale per share of Arvind Ltd., then we get NSPS = 209.29, and current market price of 05 May 2017 is 408. So please remember we use net sale per share to identify undervalued stocks. It does not mean that any stock is not traded above its net sale per share. You may also watch my YouTube video to learn more about net sale per share, here is the link: https://www.youtube.com/watch?v=1rdWmenk_wM 'Or simply search Mahesh Kaushik Net Sale Per Share' YouTube.

Summary

1. When the total number of shares divided by last quarter net sales data (net income or net revenue) of your company, this ratio is called the net sale per share for a quarter. Multiply this by 4, and this is our estimated net sale per year.
2. Do not look at net profits of a company. Always look at the net revenue of the company.
3. Choose stocks which have higher net revenue per share.
4. Buy when the market price of a stock is below its one-year net revenue per share. And sell when a stock's current market price crosses one-year net revenue per share.

❒

6

Fundamental Calculation for Predicting Target Price of Any Stock

In the last chapter, you have learnt how to identify cheap stocks with the help of net sale per share. Some followers mail to me that 'Net sale per share of Infosys is Rs. 258.12 and stock traded at Rs. 1278, how is it possible'? I again clarify that many stocks traded above its net sale per share, we use net sale per share of identified undervalued stocks. If Infosys net sale per share is Rs. 258 and stock traded @ Rs. 1278, then it simply indicates that stock is overvalued at price of Rs. 1278 and this is not a right time to buy this stock. For example, I identified Maruti share in 2005 as an undervalued stock. The 2005 price of Maruti Suzuki share was near 450 and CMP in 2017 near 6600. Now in this chapter, I tell you how to identify the target of any stock. Most investors don't know about the fundamental targeting of stocks. Many books available about the stock market teach us only about technical analysis and technical targets of stock, but no one teaches us fundamental targeting of a stock. So in this book, I will tell you my unique method of predicting fundamental target of a stock.

1. For calculating the fundamental target, first of all, check yearly net revenue per stock and note it down in a diary. Suppose company A had a net revenue of Rs. 1000 crore last year, and the total number of stocks in

company A is ten crore, then net revenue per stock per year is 1000/10 = 100, so note down 100. (In Lesson 4 of this book, I have described to you the net revenue per share concept 'When last quarter's net sales data (net income or net revenue) of your company is divided by the total number of shares, this ratio is called net sale per share for a quarter. Multiply this by four, then this is our estimated "Net sale per year"'. For more details, read lesson 4 of this book).

2. The book value of a stock is a great fundamental term. So, now that you have noted down the book value of this stock in your diary, suppose your company A's book value is 67.
3. Now check three years' DMA (a Base price which I described earlier in the 2nd lesson of this book) and suppose it is 85.
4. Now take an average of our first figure 100 (Net yearly revenue per stock) and second 67 (book value) and third 85 (base price) which works out to 100 + 67 + 85 = 252/3 = 84.
5. For best results, reduce 10% of this figure as market fluctuation correction, so 10% of 84 is 8.40; now, you can assume your fundamental target at 84.00 – 8.40 = 75.60.
6. So if the stock traded below 75.60, then it is your buy, and in more than 80% cases, I see that stock achieves this target in 1 year to 3 years. Always set your fundamental target before you buy, and it must be 15% higher than your buying rate.

Summary

1. Take averaged out net revenue per share, book value and the base price of the stock, and then reduce it by

10%. This is the fundamental target of stock.

2. Buy below 15% of the fundamental target for making profits.
3. If the stock is traded 20% or more above its fundamental target, then it should be strictly avoided.

This book contains theory, and I know my readers might feel bored when they read theory. so, I uploaded some YouTube videos to clear every concept, you may search 'fundamental target price Mahesh Kaushik' on YouTube to find my video about this chapter. Directly open from this link: https://www.youtube.com/watch?v=vsrNYQ9ToJM. 'Always set your fundamental target before you buy, and it must be 15% higher than your buying price'.

❐

7
How to Identify Speculations in a Stock

Now you select your stock which traded 20% lower or higher from base price which traded below its fundamental target price, but before you buy, first check bulk deals. Because when anything good or wrong is going to happen, news of this future incident may leak to operators and this rumour makes stock price unstable.

How to identify operator's activity in stocks?

It is very simple to identify the operator's activity in stock because they buy and sell in big lots and this big buying and selling are known as bulk or block deals in stock market language. Bulk deals mean major broker-dealers often provide 'block trading' services, sometimes known as 'upstairs trading desks' to their institutional clients. A block trade is a permissible, non-competitive, privately negotiated transaction either at or exceeding an exchange determined minimum threshold quantity of shares, which is executed apart and away from the open outcry or electronic markets. In the United States and Canada, a block trade is usually at least 10,000 shares of stock or $200,000 of bonds but in practice, significantly larger. Every stock exchange provides a history of these big deals, so if you want to identify the operator's activity in stock, visit the stock exchange website, see bulk and block deals history. You should avoid the stock if you find any big deals in the recent 24 months. Some of the stock exchanges provide big deals every day but don't provide a history of these deals. In this case, you need to start a diary for this bulk and block deals. When your data or operator activity stocks are ready, use my general criteria. I always avoid stocks which record bulk and block deals in the last two years because we are not elephants; we are small investors like ants. Operators speculate in stocks. They buy or sell huge quantities in a particular stock for increasing volume and trader's activity. At least they book profits when the stock trades at very high prices, but small investors will be trapped. If you remember and follow this trick, then you will never be trapped at a higher price. You may also check stock exchange website for past bulk/block deals, and if you find the history of bulk/block deals on the exchange website, then you need not maintain a daily diary for such types of deals.

Summary

1. Try to understand speculation of pricing in stock markets.
2. Avoid a stock which has a recent bulk (block) deal.
3. In my criteria of the stock screening, I always avoid a stock which has had a bulk deal in the last two years. (For trading stocks, I reduced this time frame from last two years to last one year).
4. When bulk deals happen in any stock which traded near its year-high and all-time high, then a downturn in this stock may be starting in the coming 1-2 months.

❐

8
Is It Good to Buy a Stock Below Face Value?

Most of the investors like stock below face value. When I was a newbie in the share market, I tried this concept many times on my penny share investing but I found that if I bought 20 penny stocks with a market price below face value, then 4-5 stocks perform well and give us more than 25% return in 3-12 months, but the other 15-16 stocks have turned out as a bad investment and showed no movement in price. The overall performance of stock below face value is not very good. So I think before you try to buy this type of stocks (stocks traded below face value), you must consider seven points of checking:

1. Promoter's holding is more than 15%.
2. Book value is not more than three times of stock current market price. Please also avoid stock with negative book value.
3. The 52-week high/low ratio is less than two.
4. The stock traded below its one-year net sale per share.
5. The stock hasn't traded 20% above its base price.
6. No recent bulk deal in the last two years.
7. No recent stock split and bonus in the last two years.
8. Stock must be traded above its 200 DMA.

If this type of stock (whose market price is less than face

value) has more than 30% promoters holding, high book value and 52-weeks' high are near market price. (In a range of 10-20% discount on 52-weeks' high), then it is good. If the stock traded at 60-80% discount on the 52-weeks' high, then this is a sign of long-term sideways movement that means based on my experience, this type of stock doesn't perform well in a 1-2 year time frame.

Summary

1. Buying a stock below its face value is not a good idea.
2. If a stock traded below its face value but promoters' holdings are good and stock reaches near its year-high (from lower price to upper price), then you can buy a stock below face value.
3. Stock below face value is risky, so always check other fundamental points like base price, one-year net revenue per share, recent bulk deals, recent stock split and bonus before you buy.

❐

9

How to Choose a Stock for Investment

In the last seven chapters of this book, you have learnt about the first theory of stock market investment that makes a diversified portfolio when the market is down. Now, you probably have a question like 'How do I choose a Stock for Investment?' So in this chapter, I will tell you about some stock screening criteria.

1. Face Value: Face value is your basic amount which you invest in the company, in other words, face value is your real share in the company's equity capital, for example if a company has 10,00,000 shares of Rs.10 face value, then share capital of the company is 10,00,000×10 = 1,00,00,000, and if you buy 50 shares of this company at the market price of Rs. 100 then you invest 50×100 = 5,000 but your partnership in company share capital is 50×10 = 500 only, the remaining Rs. 4500 is given as a premium to the seller who sells its stocks to you. If you buy a stock at Rs. 3500 whose face value is one rupee, then your investment in the company is only Rs. 1, and the remaining Rs. 3499 is a premium to the seller. Suppose, I want to buy an infra stock and choose three stock names A, B and C for screening. Suppose, the face value of A-stock is Rs. 10 and market price is 68, the face value of B-stock is Rs. 2, and market price is 48 and the face value of C-stock is Rupee 1, and market price is 12.

Which stock is cheapest in A, B or C?

Now, we compare stock market price at Rs. 1 face value, so we divide each stock market price by its face value. So in a similar face value of Rupee 1, market price for A stock is 68/10 = 6.80, for B stock 48/2 = 24 & for C stock 12/1 = 12, so stock A is the cheapest stock.

2. Year-High And Year-Low: Now, I see a year high and year-low for each stock and if the stock is down more than 50% from a year-high, then I avoid this stock. For example, year-high of stock A is 256.55, year's low is 96 and the stock traded at 108.55, then I avoid this stock because good companies never go down more than 50% within a year unless something is wrong. On the other hand, a stock is trading more than 100% from year-low, then I avoid it for example company B is traded at 56 and year-high for this company is 65.25, & year-low is 19.55, then I avoid it because I think this stock is already running very fast and it is better to wait for the market fall.

3. Promoter's Holding: If the promoter is holding 15-20%, then I think the stock is not good for investing; if the promoter holding is reduced in the last one to four quarters, then I think something is wrong and avoid this type of stock because promoters are selling their stocks to retail investors, but if promoters increase their holding, then I think it is good because promoters know this company's fundamentals very well.

One of my followers from U.S.A wrote to me 'I don't quite understand your promoters' holding concept because of the difference in the Indian market and the U.S. market. Please give me an example of what a "promoter" would mean or be in the U.S.A.'.

So I also want to tell you the meaning of a promoter, 'A promoter is a person who is engaged in the formation of the company. For example, Bill Gates is a promoter of Microsoft, and a promoter of Facebook is Mark Zuckerberg'.

4. Base Price: Finally I check the base price of the stock; this is a new concept which replaces my old criteria of 200 DMA and book value because I think base price is more reliable and more stable. If a stock just crosses its base price in upside and traded 10-20% higher than the base price, then I think buying price is a good value to buy. But on the opposite, if a stock crosses its base price in downside, then it is risky to buy. I have written a separate article about the calculation of base price in this book; so please read it for greater understanding about base price.

5. Net Revenue Per Share: Calculate the net revenue per year of stock as I described earlier in this book; if your stock price is lower than your stock valuation, it is good and if CMP is higher than it, then the stock is traded at a higher valuation.

6. No Recent Bulk Deal And No Recent Bonus: As I told you in chapter 6 of this book that a bulk deal is a sign of speculative activity, so generally, I avoid a stock which has had a recent bulk deal in the last two years.

Similarly in chapter 10 of this book, you will learn that bonus and stock splits do not change a company's fundamentals; they have only a psychological effect on investors and after a recent bonus and stock split, the stock will enter a downturn, so avoid a stock which had a recent bonus and split issue in the last 2 years.

Summary

1. When you compare prices of the two stocks, always look at their face value for identifying which stock is cheaper.
2. Do not buy if a stock falls more than 50% from the year-high.

3. Do not buy if a stock rises more than 100% from year-low.
4. Always avoid a stock which promoters are holding below 15%, and where promoters have reduced their holdings in the last one year.
5. Avoid a stock which traded 20% above its base price.
6. Choose a stock which traded below its one-year net revenue per share.
7. Avoid a stock which has a recent bulk deal in the last two years.
8. Avoid a stock which has had a recent stock split and bonus in last two years.

❐

10
Bonus and Stock Splits Give Only Psychological Effect for Investors

The bonus does not change company fundamentals and only creates a psychological effect for investors. I will clarify this, suppose one company has a total of 100 shares, and the company earns 1000 rupees in a year. Then EPS of the company is 1000/100 = 10, okay.

Now the company declares bonus 1:4, that means if you hold four shares, the company gives four shares to you free. So the total number of shares after the bonus issue has increased from 100 to 500 but the profit of the company is still 1000; so after bonus, EPS of the company is 1000/500 = 2 means that EPS is diluted after the bonus, and you see a price adjustment after bonus.

So, the bonus is beneficial only when the profit of the company increases, otherwise it will dilute the EPS and give a negative effect on long-term share price but in the short-term, if the company declares bonus, the demand of the general public increases because they do not understand that this is an equity dilution and for any increase in equity they think company is just giving them free shares.

So the price increases in the short-term but after bonus news has cooled down and adjusted itself like Unitech stock (Unitech is an Indian stock whose price came down from 12,000 to 28 after bonus and split issue).

Historically, big IT companies, Infosys and Wipro rise after the bonus issue because their profit is rising and EPS is rising. So don't try to compare every company with the big bonuses.

Summary

1. After a bonus issue and split in the face value, the number of stocks rises, so company's net EPS is diluted after the bonus.
2. Bonus and the stock split are not a big change for buying a stock.
3. After a bonus and split, investors may sell their extra stocks, so stock shows a downside after a bonus and face value split.

❐

11
Reverse Trading System

The reverse trading system is my special system to avoid loss in the stock market. This system of reverse trading is also known as delivery base short selling in the cash market. Short selling is allowed on Intraday trading and in future and option, but in this chapter, I tell you how a small investor can get the benefit of short selling in delivery base cash market investing.

For understanding, the reversal trading system, look at my example.

On 31 December 2007, when the Indian market traded at its all-time high, I bought an infra stock named Punj Lloyd which traded at 560 Indian rupees. I bought ten stocks and invested 5600 rupees in Punj Lloyd stock.

After that, the markets crashed badly and when the stock crashed more than 50% from its year-high within a year (in earlier articles of this book, I have already told you to avoid a stock which is crashing more than 50% within a year), I sold these 10 stocks of Punj Lloyd @256 and got Rs. 2560. My friends thought that I booked my loss of 5600 – 2560 = 3040 in Indian currency. But I always tell my friends that I have never booked losses in the stock market, then they wonder about my pride and want to clarify this loss-making a trade.

After that, I tracked Punj Lloyd year-high/year-low ratio regularly, and when this ratio was stable (less than 1.5), then I bought these ten stocks again @ Rs. 56 per share so, this time, my investment is Rs. 560 only and I get back Rs. 2,000 in my reverse trading (2560 – 560 = 2000), so this minimises my earlier buying cost from 5600 to 5600 – 2000 = 3600 only.

So now I hold it, and my holding cost for these 10 Punj Lloyd stocks is 3600, it means if I sell these stocks at 444 rupees per share, then I earn my 15% profit target without any loss. I will clarify it again for you.

1. First buying of Punj Lloyd 10 shares @ Rs. 560 total investment 5600.
2. Reverse sell @ Rs. 256-total losses Rs. 3040 but get Rs. 2560 back.
3. Again buy ten shares @ Rs. 56 total investment Rs. 560, so I get Rs. 2,000 cashback in this trading; it will minimise my earlier purchasing cost from Rs. 5600 to Rs. 5600 – 2000 = Rs. 3600 only.
4. Now my holding cost is Rs. 5600 – 2000 = 3600.
5. My price target is 444, so if I get it, then it will give me 444 × 10 = 4440, so I get 4440 – 3600 = 840 rupees as my 15% profit.

I repeat it in another way. I started with an investment of Rs. 5600.

First Trading:

1. Bought 10 shares @ Rs. 560 = 5600
2. Sold @ Rs. 256 = 2560
3. Loss of Rs. 5600 – 2560 = Rs. 3040

Once the correction happened, and Rs. stock stabled, the amount I am left with from the first transaction is only Rs. 2560.

Second Trading:

Bought the same quantity of 10 shares @ Rs. 56

1. Bought 10 shares @ Rs. 56 = 560.

2. Remaining amount = Rs. 2000 (2560 – 560).

3. If I sell the stock @ Rs. 444, I will get money back of Rs. 4440.

Adding these (4440 + 2000) gives me back Rs. 6440.

Combining both tradings, I got Rs. 6440 back from the initial amount; I started with Rs. 5600 and profit is Rs. 840, which is 15% of Rs. 5600.

Okay, I still hold these ten shares because, Punj Lloyd traded below my target price Rs. 444.

So when you are trapped in a loss-making trade, track its year-high or year-low ratio. When a stock crash is more than 50% from the year-high, it means year-high or year-low ratio is more than two, so this is a sign of long-term bearish trend, then it is wise to book your loss.

And after some years when the downturn in particular script is stable, means year-high/year-low ratio is less than 1.5, this time, you will buy your same quantity again. Update of the new edition: If you read my recent book 'How Chandu Earned And Chinki Lost In The Stock Market'?, then you may be familiar with this new update. Here, I provide some outline for new readers who have not read the book yet. (However, it is recommended that you read 'How Chandu Earned and Chinki Lost in the Stock Market'? book for a deeper understanding of this update).

Now I update this reverse trading system, and you simply need to track 200 DMA of your portfolio stocks. You can calculate 200 DMA by yourself and find it on Moneyeontrot site or watch my YouTube video about 200 DMA calculating:

https://www.youtube.com/watch?v=rSVbuSddVBU. Do not buy a stock which traded below this 200 DMA. If stock traded above 200 DMA, then hold it. When a stock closes below 5% of 200 DMA, then it is a sign of selling your stock either for profit or the loss. Because in more than 90% cases, I find if stock closes 5% or more below 200 DMA, then it enters a long-term downtrend so if you sell your stock on this break even point, then you may protect your investments from further downside. When correction is over, and your stock closes at 5% above 200 DMA, then buy the same quantity again.

With the help of this method, you consider closing –5% below 200 DMA as a stop-loss. So when you sell your stock 5% below 200 DMA and buy 5% above 200 DMA again, then actually you do not book your loss, you simply use the reverse trading system. Kindly read my recent book 'How Chandu Earned And Chinki Lost In The Stock Market'? for a more deeper understanding of this update.

Summary

1. Reverse trading may protect your money from loss.
2. When you are trapped in a loss-making investment, then track its year-high/year-low ratio; when stock crashes more than 50% from its year-high, it means year-high/year-low ratio is more than two, this is a sign of long-term bearish trend, so sell it. And after some years, when year- high/year-low ratio is less than 1.5, this time, you will buy your same quantity again.
3. When a stock closes below 5% of 200 DMA, then it is a sign of selling your stock either for profit or loss.
4. When correction is over, and your stock closes 5% above 200 DMA, then buy the same quantity again.

❑

12
My Army Method of Profit Booking in Long-Term Equity SIP

If you have fancy stock and you want to buy a huge holding in a particular stock, then I will tell you my secret method of safe investing and safe profit booking.

First of all, make a long-term equity systematic investment plan in your fancy stock, suppose you want to buy a huge holding in Country Club, then make a monthly $50 SIP in Country Club for five years.

After five years, you have a huge holding of Country Club. Now you use my unique army method for profit booking.

My Unique Army Method: For understanding this Army Method, suppose an Army Captain has 10,000 soldiers and the enemy attacks his post, so what is the right method for defence?

a. All 10,000 soldiers will fight, and if the enemy kills all of them, then you have lost your army post.

b. Divide all soldiers into ten teams of 1000 soldiers, the enemy first fights with 1000 soldiers, and if all 1000 soldiers are martyred, then the 2nd team of 1000 soldiers will fight, and if this team is also martyred, then next 3rd team will fight...till all ten teams are martyred.

1. This is not a joke I am trying to tell you about a serious method of stock market defence.

2. I think option 'b' is the best defence option for any Captain by the strategy of dividing soldiers.

3. Okay, I use the above option in my long-term SIP. Suppose, you invest $50 per month in Country Club and after five years, you have 2563 stocks and the price of Country Club is $198. Now treat each of your stocks like a soldier and divide these 2563 into ten lots of 256-256 stocks.

If the price of Country Club falls more than 30% from any nearest high (in this example, we suppose price of Country Club is $198 after 2 years) then booking your 256 stocks means if Country Club slides back from 30% of 198 and touches $ 138.60, then book your 1/10 part of holding (hold the remaining 90% shares and continue your SIP).

4. If the price falls further by 30% from here (30% of $ 138.60), then book another 256 (1/10). The supposed price is $ 198, and you can take any figure instead of $ 198; suppose you take 100, then book your first 1/10 at 70 and second at 70 – 21 (30% of 70) = 49...third 49 – 14.70 = 34.30.

5. I think you understand my Army Method of profit booking in long-term equity SIP; this is necessary to protect your profits because no one gives you the guarantee that your stock will continue upwards in the coming ten years.

Summary

1. Do not buy a huge holding in your fancy stock.
2. If any stock is your fancy, then make a long-term equity SIP in particular stock.
3. When you hold a huge quantity of any stock in profits, then do not book profit in all of your holdings.
4. Divide all of your holdings into 1/10 parts and if this stock starts falling, then sell 1/10 part at every 30% price fall.

❒

13
Golden Rules for Winning in the Stock Market

1. First of all, divide your money into two parts – 70% in equity and 30% in cash and mutual fund (like the gilt fund, debt fund or ETF).

2. Never put all of your money in a single stock and 2-10 stocks, try to be more diversified in your portfolio like a retail shop.

3. For low risk, always invest in good company share; I will give you some checkpoint for deciding a good company:

A. If one-year net revenue per share is higher than the market price.

B. If a company pays dividends, then it is good.

C. Promoters' holding in the company must be above 15%.

4. At a time purchase only the minimum quantity of a share (in the Indian market at a time purchasing of Rs. 5,000-10,000) (near $100-200) is sufficient (for fundamentally sound share) and in penny share not to invest more than Rs. 2,500-5,000 (near $40-80) rupees at a time. Do not be greedy, for example, if you have Rs. 1,00,000, first divide it in 70:30 ratio. If you have a total of Rs. 1,00,000 savings, then invest only Rs. 70,000 in equity market or hold Rs. 30,000 in bank FD or other instruments. From Rs. 70,000, you can purchase 14

companies equity shares by investing 5000 in each stock. But in a trading week, we purchase only one company because if we buy these 14 companies in 14 weeks, then we have time to do good research and chance to buy them at a low price.

5. Avoid buying in same sector company, for example, TCS or INFOSYS, both are software companies, and if both qualify in your four-point checking system which I gave in part 1, then you select only one company. How you select one of these two companies is simple. Again check both companies in our four-point checking system and which point is higher, select it.

6. Most important thing – future and option or intraday trading strictly prohibited for my followers.

If you are a short-term trader and want to make some quick money in a very short time like a day or 2-3 days, then only luck or God can save your money, and I think this book is not for you.

7. On the basis of the above rules, I think you make your best-diversified portfolio of 50-100 companies.

8. Not to average out your stock in every Rs. 5-10 fall. 'Average' out must be done when your stock closes 5% above from 200 DMA. (Read more details in Chapter 26 of this book).

9. Do not borrow money for stock market investing; as a stock market investor, it is compulsory that you are a debt-free person. If you have big debts on your credit cards and you borrow money for your needs then, first of all, please repay all of your debts and loans and then start your stock market business. If you want to start your investment with my style, I recommended you to save 10% of your monthly income and fix your first month 10% amount as your basic investment amount, suppose your monthly income is Rs. 60,000 per month, then fix 10% of 60,000 = 6000 rupees as your basic

investment amount in every stock. Every year increase 7.5% in this basic investment amount, read more details in the next chapter.

Summary

1. Don't put all of your savings in equity.
2. Invest a minimum amount in a single stock.
3. Do not trade in future and option and intraday speculation.
4. Do not average out at every fall.
5. It is compulsory to become a debt-free person before starting any stock market investment.
6. Do not borrow money for stock market investing.

❐

14
How to Increase Your Investment in the Stock Market

In an earlier chapter, I told you that if you want to invest Rs. 50,000 in the stock market, then divide it into ten lots of Rs. 5000-5000 each.

It means invest only Rs. 5000 in a single stock and hold a stock minimum of one year period and after one year if you got profit more than 15%, then sell it and book your gains.

Okay, I think you have already read this in my book.

But now I want to tell you one of my secret formulas about how I keep my mind peaceful and happy in every market condition.

In 2005, I started investing in the stock market with the basic money of Rs. 1,02,600 and bought 38 shares with investments of Rs. 2700-2700 in each company.

In 2005, when I bought my first stock, I fixed Rs. 2700 as the basic amount of every stock and increase this basic amount every year by 7.5% increment, so the year 2017 basic amount is Rs. 6400.

Suppose, I sell one of these lots in 2006 and get 15% + profit. It means my initial investment was Rs. 2700 and I got Rs. 405 profit (after reducing brokerage).

It meant after one year, my Rs. 2700 becomes 2700 + 405 = Rs. 3,105, and now I want to invest my money in a fresh stock, so what is right strategy for me?

1. Invest the entire Rs. 3,105 in new stock.
2. Or enjoy my profit of Rs. 405 and invest the basic amount Rs. 2700 again.

I know most of the readers choose option 2 for me, but both options are wrong if you want to make money in the stock market.

Now I tell you my secret formula of reinvesting.

1. If I go with option one, I never earn from the market; this option is like gambling where the gambler reinvests his entire winning amount and one day he loses all of his money.
2. In the second option, my earning and profits are always limited. Everyone wants to increase his investments; everyone wants to increase his earnings.
3. So what is the right choice? The right theory (or my theory) is that I always increase 7.5% of my basic amount when reinvesting money after profit booking.

So 7.5% of 2700 is 202.50 which I rounded off to the nearest 50 and after rounding it is 200. So my reinvestment amount is 2700 + 200 = 2900 and remaining 3105 – 2900 = 205 is my earning which I use to fulfil my needs.

4. I rotate this formula every year; means every year I again increase my reinvestment amount by 7.5% (and I rounded off to the nearest 50, so in 2017, my basic investment amount in every stock is Rs. 6400).

Watch this table to understand how I increase my investment year by year:

Year	Last Year/ Initial Amount	7.5% Increment	Increased Amount in Nearest 50	Basic Amount of Year
2005	2700	–	–	2700
2006	2700	202.5	200	2900
2007	2900	217.5	200	3100
2008	3100	232.5	250	3350
2009	3350	251.25	250	3600
2010	3600	270	250	3850
2011	3850	288.75	300	4150
2012	4150	311.25	300	4450
2013	4450	333.75	350	4800
2014	4800	360	350	5150
2015	5150	386.25	400	5550
2016	5550	416.25	400	5950
2017	5950	446.25	450	6400

5. In this example, 15% profit is minimum; sometimes I get more than 15% like 40-125% profit in my trade. In this case, I increase only 7.5% and put 7.5% in my pocket. I use the remaining profit to increase the number of lots. For example, in 2008 when the market was beaten down and most stocks traded at a very discounted price, I invested Rs. 3350 in a stock and got 125% profit (4187.50) in this trade, then I make a new lot of 3350 with my profit.

(I honestly disclose that the above investment amount examples are notional examples because in my earlier trading years of 2005-2008, I also broke discipline in investment amounts and did not strictly follow basic investment amounts.

But now I strictly follow my rules given in this book and do not invest more than Rs. 6400 in a single stock, except Country Club stock which I buy through my special SIP method which was given in my book 'How Chandu Earned, and Chinki Lost in the Stock Market').

Summary

1. Choose your initial Investment amount in each stock.
2. Book your profit when the stock has risen more than 15% and rotate your money in new stock.
3. Every time increase 7.5% in your new investment amount.

What are the basic reasons for the changing prices of stocks?

1. Two things make the market price of every stock:

(First thing) the face value of stock + (second thing) premium to the stock = market price of the stock. For example, the stock of Reliance Communication Ltd is trading at 65. The face value of this stock is 5 rupees, and market premium is 60, so the current market price is 5 + 60 = 65.

2. Face value does not change in normal trading, it is changed only if the board of directors passes a resolution for this purpose. In trading, the stock premium is only changed by demand and supply formula. Suppose, I bid for buying 1000 stocks of Reliance Communication Ltd in the open market and no one agrees to sell his stocks @65 (at a premium of 60), so the premium is increased from 60 to 61, 62, 63... and so on until circuit limit.

Suppose, one could agree to sell his stock @75 so, in this case, he gets 70 rupees premium, and if my trade is made, then the current market price is now 75; it means 70 as (premium) + 5 (face value) = 75

3. It means if I buy a stock of 5 rupees for 75 rupees, my

partnership in company equity is only 5 rupees; if a company gives 50% dividend, then it is not 75/2 = 37.50; it is 5/2 = 2.5 per stock only because I give 5 rupees to the company and 70 rupees to the seller of the stock. So my partnership with company capital is only 5 rupees.

4. When the number of buyers is higher (demand is higher) in stock, then its price is up (premium is up) and when the sellers are more (demand is down), then the price of the stock is down (premium is down).

5. No one controls the stock premium. The buyer and seller agreement decides it. Sometimes exchange fixes a circuit limit to control excess speculation in the stock price.

6. One other useful piece of information that why one could pay a premium for buying a stock? It is due to stock EPS (earnings per stock) for example, face value of XYZ stock is one rupee only but per stock earnings of XYZ stock is 4.78 so anyone gives us his stock at only one rupee (because this stock earns approximately 5 rupees a year) he gives us his stock if we give him a premium of 199 rupees, because the current market price of XYZ stock is 200 (1 + 199). It means we pay him 40 years of earnings advance to buy a stock. It is called P/E (price/earnings per stock). So P/E of XYZ stock is 40.

7. One other thing, sometimes a company has low equity like MMTC, this company has only 5,00,00,000 stock of 10 rupees face value and the promoter holds 99.33% stock, so the remaining 3,35,000 stock trade in this market; if these stocks are held by some investors and demand is still in market, then price is going higher, and higher you wonder current market price of MMTC is 32,440 and EPS is 43, so MMTC P/E is 754 (means we pay 754 year earnings to buy a stock of MMTC) (This chapter was originally written on 25.06.2010, so price given as example is for 25.06.2010).

8. The last point, the premium may be negative also. For example, Pan India Corporation Ltd. is a 10 rupees face value stock, but its current market price of 0.70 only means that a premium on this stock is -9.30.

(This chapter was originally written on 25.06.2010, so the price given for this example was 25.06.2010 price).

Summary

1. Face value and premium make the stock price.
2. The premium of shares depends on demand and supply theory.
3. So rising and downside possibility in stock is unlimited (in downside limited to zero or delisting from the exchange).

'Downside and upside possibility in stocks are unbelievable; so do not pay high premiums for stocks which you buy for trade because premiums will increase or go down rapidly when market conditions change'.

❐

15
Biggest Lie of the Share Market

One day when I went to the market to buy vegetables, my shopkeeper said to me 'Oh Sir, your market (share market) is near its all-time high, so I think you make huge profits'.

I replied, 'It is the biggest lie of share market'. He wonders 'How'?

I explained: 'Our index Nifty has 50 stocks and we changed 18 stocks in Nifty; from 2007 near about 38% shares changed in Nifty, so how as we compare 2007 Nifty to 2010 Nifty'?

From 1996 to 2017, total 172 scripts changed in Nifty.

Yes, this is true: Today, I expose this biggest lie of the market to my book readers.

This lie is 'Index is a constant variable'.

The truth is 'Index figure is not a constant figure; stocks in a stock market index are not constant. Stocks in a market index are subject to change from time to time'.

These 17 shares have changed in Nifty constitution from 4 April, 2007 to 1 October, 2010.

Date of Inclusion	Securities Included	Securities Excluded
1-Oct-10	Sesa Goa	Unitech
1-Oct-10	Dr Reddy	Idea
1-Oct-10	Bajaj Auto	ABB
8-Apr-10	Kotak Bank	Grasim
22-Oct-09	JP Associates	TATA Comm
22-Oct-09	IDFC	National Alum
17-Jun-09	Jindal Steel	RPL
27-Mar-09	Axis Bank	ZEEL
12-Jan-09	Relcapital	Satyam Comp
10-Sep-08	R Power	Dr Reddy
14-Mar-08	DLF	Glaxo
14-Mar-08	Power Grid	Bajaj Auto
12-Dec-07	Idea	MTNL
12-Dec-07	Cairn	Hind Petro
5-Oct-07	Unitech	IPCL
24-Sep-07	NTPC	Dabur
4-Apr-07	RPL	JET Airways
4-Apr-07	STER	Orient Bank

The stock market index is not the best parameter; for checking stock valuation, always see the particular share price movement not to consider index movement to evaluate a particular stock.

Update in 2017: From 18 September 1996 to 31 March 2017, Nifty constitution changed 171 times; you may download full Excel Sheet from NSE India website of these 171 changes in Nifty scripts. Here is the link to download all changes in Nifty, Nifty Junior, Nifty Midcap etc.:

https://www.nseindia.com/content/indices/IndexInclExcl.xls

I have also included an 'Appendix' in the last pages of this book, where you will find a list of the above 171 changes in Nifty.

What do you think? Has our index been a fair parameter of market health?

Mail your reply to me at mahesh2073@yahoo.com

Summary

1. Stocks in a market index are changed from time to time.
2. So the stock market index is not the best parameter; for checking stocks' valuation, always see particular share price movement, not to consider index movement.
3. In my personal experience at every index level, some of the companies' stocks perform well; so if you have a diversified portfolio, then you have a chance to sell and get 15% profits at every level of the market index.
4. Nifty stocks changed 171 times after 1996.

❐

16
What is Option Trading?

I would not like to advise you to trade in the F&O segment in the stock market because F&O is a tool for the big institutional investor. I include this article in this book for the educational purpose of small investors.

An option is a contract, which gives the buyer the right, but not the obligation to buy or sell shares of the underlying security at a specific price on or before a specific date.

There are two kinds of options: Call Option and Put Option.

A Call Option is an option to buy a stock at a specific price on or before a certain date. When you buy a Call Option, the price you pay for it, called the option premium, secures your right to buy that certain stock at a specified price called the strike price. If you decide not to use the option to buy the stock, and you are not obligated to, your only cost is the option premium.

For example, suppose Praveen Goswami purchases one Infosys Computer DEC 2350 Call at a premium of 20. This contract allows Praveen Goswami to buy 100 shares of Infosys at Rest 2350 per share at any time between the current date and the end of December. For this privilege, Praveen Goswami pays a fee of Rest 2000 (Rest 20 a share for 100 shares). The buyer of a call has purchased the right to buy, and for that, he pays a premium. Now let us see how one can profit from buying an option.

If the stock rises above Rest 2370 (2350 + 20), he will break even, and he will start making a profit. Suppose, the stock does not rise and instead falls, he will choose not to exercise the option and forego the premium of Rest 20, thereby limiting his loss of Rest 2000.

When you expect prices to rise, then you take a long position by buying calls. You are bullish.

When you expect prices to fall, then you take a short position by selling calls. You are bearish.

Put Options are options to sell a stock at a specific price on or before a certain date. With a Put Option, you can 'ensure' stock by fixing a selling price. If something happens which causes the stock price to fall, and thus, 'damages' your asset, you can exercise your option and sell it at its 'insured' price level. If the price of your stock goes up, and there is no 'damage', then you do not need to use the insurance, and, once again, your only cost is the premium.

For example, Satya purchases one Infosys Technologies DEC 2350 Put-Premium 20. This contract allows Satya to sell 100 shares INTEC at Rest 2350 per share at any time between the current date and the end of August. To have this privilege, Sam pays a premium of Rest 2000 (Rest 20 a share for 100 shares). The buyer of a Put has purchased a right to sell. The owner of a Put Option has the right to sell. So he will break even only after the stock falls below Rest 2330 (2350-20) and will start making a profit if the stock falls below Rest 2330.

This is the primary function of listed options, to allow investors ways to manage risks.

The Strike Price denotes the price at which the buyer of the option has a right to purchase or sell the underlying. Five different strike prices will be available at any point in time. The strike price interval will be about 20. The strike price is also called Exercise Price. This price is fixed by the exchange for the entire duration of the option depending on the movement of the underlying stock or index in the cash market.

Now we come to our main point: 'Please note that future and option are not for small investors like you and me, they are useful tools for big players like mutual funds and FII, but if a small player plays this game, then he/she will always lose their hard earned money. I have never seen a small investor make permanent big money from F&O; he enjoys speculation for some time and then ends up losing all of his money in F&O'.

Summary

1. Future and options trading is not for small investors; it is a tool for big institutional investors and speculators.
2. So it is wise to avoid future and option, and Intraday trading for protecting your hard-earned money.

❒

17
How Analysts on TV Confuse Us?

Before you continue with this chapter, please note that every analyst on TV is not wrong, but we understand their technical language incorrectly because technical terms work fine for traders only if you are an investor; then, investing by fundamentals is a good theory.

For example, Rita from Delhi buys 1000 ITC shares with Rs. 2.20 lakh at the rate of Rs. 220 per share in the year 2005. when she hears that ITC share is continuing in an uptrend and in last 2 years ITC share price has reached 220 from 70. She also hears a technical analyst on TV say that the chart pattern of this share is very good and in the long-term uptrend.

If share price crosses 250, then it goes to 400, and the next target is 600 then 1000. She also hears a fundamental analyst say that it is a blue chip company in FMCG business and grew 20-30% every year so if you invest in the long-term horizon, you will get a decent return.

After her investment share goes to 240, she cannot sell and book profit because she has a long-term horizon. Then shares come down to 200, she averages it out and buys 500 more shares (1.10 lakh rupees). Then share goes to 150 and trades as 150 to 180 in the year 2006 and 2007 respectively.

when she got no return on her investment, then she asked the same technical analyst on TV about her investment. He replies that why did she not follow a stop-loss of Rs. 200? If the share is in a downtrend, book your loss and go to a technically sound share like Reliance, whose shares trade at Rs. 3000 and our price target is Rs. 4500 in one year.

After shifting, Reliance goes to 1200 and ITC goes to 350.

However, Rita says goodbye to the share market forever, and she always criticises stock market and its speculation.

Summary

1. Do not blindly follow every analyst on TV. Apply your common sense before investing.
2. Try to understand differences of a short-term technical tip and long-term fundamental investing.
3. Swapping from a loss-making stock to another stock is not a good policy.

❐

18
Spiritual Tips for Traders

Now we discuss the market from a spiritual viewpoint. The market depends on three planets Surya (Sun), Rahu and Shani (Saturn). So sometimes you experience the unwanted loss in your market trades. And you see your friend who has less experience, whose trading pattern is foolish and risky but he makes a profit on every trade, and you make a loss on every trade.

Astrologer says it is due to a planetary pattern in the horoscope. Some Gujarati traders on the market always consult their astrologers before making any trading decisions.

Do you believe these things or not?

Okay, in my view, these things are right, and I believe in these tools.

Today I will tell you a simple *Totka* (spiritual formula) to control your loss in the market. But this is only to share my view with other investors; please do not speculate blindly in the market because of this tip. Otherwise, I am not liable for any loss because there are no guarantees and no scientific reason that this tip is footproof.

But it is not a bad idea to try this and make comments about whether it is working or not working.

This is the spiritual formula – On Tuesday, take a small piece (near about 3-7 inches) of *shisham* (Dalbergia Sissoo) tree bark. Wash it with fresh water and dry it. Always keep this bark in your pocket when you work in the market. There is a saying that it will help in making sound decisions in the market and relax your mind when you trade and increase your level of confidence. It is also said that it will help you to make the winning decision. Try it and report comments about what differences you observe in your trades after using this tip.

Tree of Dalbergia Sissoo, best of luck. Please read the disclaimer before making any trade. The author is not liable for any loss and no there is guarantee of this tip.

Summary

1. It is believed that if a trader keeps Dalbergia *Sissoo* tree bark in his pocket, then he will be lucky in trading.
2. Our small investor also tries this tip when he goes to a place to buy or sell order in the market and keeps Dalbergia Sissoo bark in the pocket for better luck.

❐

19
Easy Technical Analysis for Small Investors

If you want to learn technical analysis of stocks but find it difficult, then do not worry, you are in the right place. I write these points in simple language for small investors and day traders, who feel uneasy about learning technical analysis of stocks. so read the following points carefully and learn step by step simple technical analysis:

1. Technical analysis is a chart reading technique and method of evaluating stocks by analysing statistics generated by market activity, past prices and volume.
2. I do not teach you how to draw charts and how to calculate the RSI, moving average etc. Because in this computer age, you will find 100 sites that will instantly draw a stock chart for you. Therefore, we will learn chart reading in the simplest possible way.
3. The stock opened at (or near) its low and closed near its high is a bullish pattern. Suppose Infosys share closed at 1190.55 and its day low is 1185.02 and day high is 1210.33, next day opens at 1184.35 and make a high 1225.33 and finally closed at 1217.52, then it is a bullish pattern, and you go long in this stock.
4. That the stock opened at (or near), it was high and dropped substantially to close near its low, is a bearish

pattern. Moreover, if in the above example, share opens at 1212.55 and closes at 1187.22, then it is a bearish pattern, and you go short on this stock.

5. If a stock trades above its 50-day or 100-day moving average, it is a bullish pattern and you can hold or ride your stock.
6. If a stock trades below its 50-day or 100-day moving average, then it is a bearish pattern, and you book your profit or loss.
7. See RSI (Relative Strength Index) on your chart if RSI is above 70, then the stock is overbought and risky, and you are not to trade long with such type of stock and book your profit. Moreover, if RSI is less than 30, then you start your investing.
8. Resistance is a price level above the current market price, at which selling pressure should be strong enough to overcome buying pressure and thus keep the price from going any higher. So book your profit before resistance.
9. Support is a price level below the current market price, at which buying interest should be able to overcome selling pressure and thus keep the price from going any lower. So start buying above support.

I think these 9 points are helpful for a small investor to find stock movement and remember technical analysis is not always right, so try some fundamental quarries also.

Summary

1. It is necessary for a small investor to keep some knowledge of technical analysis but always invest in fundamentals.
2. Before investing, please check moving averages, RSI, support and resistance to make a good decision.

❒

20
My Basic Concepts for Investing in Penny Stocks

One day my boss (I work in the *Tehsil* office, so *Tehsildar* is my boss) asked me why I dislike penny stocks. He suggested to me that one could trade in these penny stocks like a scrap business. He advised me to visit a scrap shop and interview the shopkeeper. Fortunately, I met a scrap business person (in Hindi called *kabaria*) and asked him how much he earns with scrap. He told me that it is simple; he bought scrap nearly free because he bought an iron scrap @ Rs. 5 per kg and sold it ten times higher @ Rs. 50 in Delhi scrap market. He told me that he makes about a 1000% margin in scrap trading. So I think seriously about starting my share scrap business (means start trading in penny stocks). Because only penny stocks give you amazing returns and our wanted 15% profit is easier with a low price stock.

How to Choose a Good Penny Stock?

Penny stocks are like scrap because most of the companies, the stock of which is traded at such a low price are sick units. So choosing a sound penny stock is a difficult job.

Today I tell you some of my criteria to choose a good penny stock for my investment.

I follow these rules strictly for investing in a penny share:

1. It's year-high or year-low ratio is not more than 2

(two), described earlier in this book.

2. Its promoters' holding must be more than 20%, and promoters should not be reducing their holdings in the last one year.
3. Its market price is less than one year. Net revenue per share and net sales or net revenue is not nil.
4. There is no recent stock split or bonus issue activity in the last three years because in most of the stock split and bonus stocks, they do not move again for nearly 3-5 years.
5. No bulk deals in the last two years.

I scan many penny companies per day for my investment, and if I find any companies that meet all of these criteria, then I make a very small investment in these penny stocks.

Summary

1. Invest only 10% of your total investment amount in penny stocks because they are risky.
2. Penny stocks may give you multiple returns if you choose a good penny stock.
3. Penny stocks are like scrap because most of the companies whose stock traded at such a low price are sick units. So choosing a sound penny stock is a difficult job.

❒

21
The Formula for Short-Term Trading

First of all, I tell my readers that I always avoid intraday trading. This formula is not given here for intraday trading, but it is useful for 7-30 days delivery-based trading and future and options positions.

Why do I give this formula in my book which is only for investors?

I give this formula here because if any trader buys my book, then he gets the value of its buying price and is educated to recognise a short period rise and fall signs in stocks.

Now I tell you the theory of intraday chart reading or some technical analysis for trading in stocks.

This formula is popular among my friends under the name of 'share genius formula of intraday trading'.

This is a simple formula (simplicity is my speciality) –take the last day open, and close prices, then reduce open prices and close prices and note down this entry and whether it is a negative figure or a positive figure. Then check the next day open price again reduce it with last days close price and note down the result as a negative figure or positive figure.

Okay, now remember this share genius formula of day trading.

1. If last close – last open = negative figure and last close – today open is also a negative figure, then you may make short positions because the stock is bearish.

2. If last close – last open = positive figure and last close – today open is also a positive figure, then you may make long positions because the stock is bullish.

For example, see this price data of Arvind Ltd.

Check data of 17 December 2012, and 18 December 2012, price data of 17 December 2012 closed – 17 December 2012 open is 92. 95 – 90.95 = 2 is a positive figure, and 17 December, 2012 close – 18 December, 2012 open is 93.25 – 92.95 = 0.30 is also a positive figure, so you may take a long position in Arvind on 18 December 2012 (market proved this, and you got a target of 106 after this bullish sign).

Now check 11 January 2013 and 14 January 2013 ratio (market closed on 12 and 13 January 2013).

11 January 2013 close – 11 January 2013 open is 102.80 – 103.7 = (–) 0.90 is a negative figure and 11 January 2013 close – 14 January 2013 open is 102.80 – 103 = (–) 0.20 this is also a negative figure and market proves this because on 19 January 2013 Arvind Ltd. fell to near 96. This formula has given us 70-80% accuracy for making a short or long position.

New Update: Above short-term trading, the formula was invented by me in 2010, but after more experience and more research, I find that if we make one change in this formula, then it is useful for day trading.

Here is the modified formula for day trading:

1. If last close – last open = negative figure and today open – the last close is also a negative figure, then you may make short positions because the stock is bearish.
2. If last close – last open = positive figure and today open – the last close is also a positive figure, then you may make long positions because the stock is bullish.

You may use the modified formula for day trading.

For intraday trading first, select any ten stocks which traded above its 200 DMA and 30 DMA.

You may find 200 DMA and 30 DMA on money-control site, no need to calculate it.

Now run this formula in above ten stocks which you select.

You find 3-4 stocks which fulfil this condition

Last close – last open = positive figure and today open – the last close is also a positive figure.

Make a long position in these three stocks but use 30 DMA as your stop-loss. You find that you make profits in 70-90% trade.

For short positions, first, select any ten stocks which traded below its 200 DMA and 30 DMA.

You may find 200 DMA and 30 DMA on money-control site no need to calculate it.

Now run this formula in above ten stocks which you select.

You find 3-4 stocks which fulfil this condition:

Last close – last open = negative figure and today open – the last close is also a negative figure.

Make a short position in these three stocks but use 30 DMA as your stop-loss. You find that you make profits in 70-90% trade.

Summary

1. For 2-30 Days Positional calls, use this formula:

(A) If last close – last open = negative figure and last close – today open is also a negative figure, then you may make short positions because the stock is bearish.

(B) If last close – last open = positive figure and last close – today open is also a positive figure, then you may make long positions, because the stock is bullish.

But choose stocks which traded above 200 DMA and use 200 DMA as stop-loss.

For Intraday Calls, use this formula:

(A) If last close – last open = negative figure and today open – the last close is also a negative figure, then you may make short positions because the stock is bearish.

(B) If last close – last open = positive figure and today open – the last close is also a positive figure, then you may make long positions because the stock is bullish. But choose stocks which traded above 30 DMA and 200 DMA and use 30 DMA as stop-loss.

❐

22
Mutual Fund Investing

I do not invest in mutual funds because I think when we invest in mutual funds, we lose the chance of learning about markets and miss the excitement of direct investing.

When I invest directly in stock and stock runs above 25%, I feel very excited and find more happiness in my research. But in mutual funds, I feel they run very slowly and as per market only. If the market runs 20-25%, they run 30% but when the market is down 15%, they also go down 15-20%.

I wonder why that expert on TV always suggests a stop-loss theory but why stop-loss doesn't apply to mutual funds? Why funds NAV fall as per market? In 2007 market, correct 60% and NAV of all mutual funds also gets corrected by 50-70%. So my question is 'Why don't they apply stop-loss like a small investor? If they apply stop-loss at 15-20% falling, then its NAV does not fall more than 20%'.

So, generally, I avoid mutual funds, but I like to make a single SIP in the largest corpus-size fund for making secure profits (and use my profit-booking formula in this SIP, which I will tell you later in this book).

My criteria to choose a Mutual Fund

1. Most of my followers ask me about the best tax saving plan in a mutual fund. I think you knew that my view is always different from normal advisors because I have the reasons to justify my views.

2. Normal advisors and business books take the criteria of past performance of a mutual fund; so every year, they change their top picks and advise small investors to shift their money from one fund to another fund because past performance is not guaranteed and always change from fund to fund and time to time.
3. But my criteria are more steady and stable for long periods.
4. I choose mutual fund schemes 'which have largest fund size' because I believe the scheme with largest fund size is a market leader and fund managers have more money to diversify the portfolio to give stable returns for investors.

Summary

1. Mutual fund investment is a passive investment.
2. Invest only in SIP method.
3. Choose fund which has largest corpus size. The scheme with the largest corpus-size is a market leader, and the fund manager has more money to diversify its portfolio to give stable returns for investors.
4. Do not forget to book timely profits in your mutual fund SIP.
5. Advice based on past performance may be changed every time, so do not swap your largest corpus-size fund with any other more performing fund, because long-term largest corpus size fund will win.

❐

23

Choose Dividend Option in ELSS

When you invest in mutual funds for saving income tax (in some countries like India, investment in equity-linked saving schemes are tax-free), then your units of ELSS (equity linked saving schemes) are locked for three years. So if you choose the dividend option on ELSS, then you will enjoy dividends every year on your locked units of ELSS. Remember dividends on mutual fund units are tax-free in some countries. So, in my theory, choose a dividend option of equity-linked saving mutual fund scheme with a lock-in period and invest in a systematic investment plan (invest in equal monthly instalments).

Summary

1. Choose the dividend option in ELSS because dividends are tax-free (in India) so you enjoy a dividend in your lock-in period.
2. In ELSS, invest only in SIP method.

❐

24
How to Book Profits in Mutual Fund SIP

When the market is in bullish trend, most investors do not book their profit from their mutual funds because they are confused by TV channels where the expert says the India growth story is a long-term story of 20-30 years so this is the time to buy and hold (in 2007, this line was common on TV), and when the market crashed in 2008, they lost all of their unrealised profits.

So I invented a formula to book profits in long-term mutual fund systematic investment plans.

1. This is a very simple but very powerful formula to book profit in an SIP of a mutual fund. You may apply it to any fund history.
2. I think you will like it very much because I invented this formula from hard research work on the history of mutual funds.
3. In this formula, when your total portfolio value grows 11%, then book your 33% corpus and continue your SIP.
4. For example, you start an SIP of 500 rupees in a mutual fund at NAV of 10 After 15 months of your SIP, suppose your total units are 733, total investments 15 × 500 = 7500 and now NAV is 11.36, so the current value of

your portfolio is 11.36 × 733 = 8326.88.

Now your net profit is 8326.88 – 7500 = 826.88; it is above 11% of your desired profit, so now book your 1/3 (33%) holding which means you hold 733 units, so you sell 733/3 = 244.33 unit it will give you 244.33 × 11.36 = 2775.58, in this 2775.58 you assume that you book all of your profit 826.88 and the remaining 2775.58 – 826.88 = 1948.70 is principal investment which you book as profit.

Now your remaining investment in SIP is 7500 – 1948.70 = 5551.30. Now continue your SIP, adding per month 500 in principal amount and wait for the next 11% rise in total investment.

About the formula given above, one of my readers e-mailed me that 'Dear Mahesh, I have been reading your posts for a long time. I have prepared an Excel Sheet for your profit booking formula, which was earlier mentioned in your blog. (Book profit with 1/3 of total units/shares held when profit reaches a certain level). I want to share it with you to know if there exists any discrepancy because I do not find the same results as yours'.

I checked this reader's sheet and found that he does not reduce the principal amount after profit-booking and forgets to reduce the principal amount after profit-booking.

I think now you understand that when your investment is growing 11%, you may book 1/3rd of holding and after deduction of 11% profit, enjoy remaining principal amount for your personal use and debt funds.

It will secure your realised profits from any market fall and also balance your portfolio in debt and equity because my advice is to use your principal amount (which you get in profit booking) in debt instruments like FD or saving account, where you will also get 5-7% annual interest on this principal amount.

Summary

1. Do not forget to book profit in mutual fund SIP.
2. It will secure your realised profits from any market fall and also balance your portfolio in debt and equity.

❒

25
Criteria to Hold a Stock

Now, I want to tell you my criteria to hold a stock beyond 15% profit. If stock price goes up with volumes and market conditions are favourable for your stock, then hold it.

Normally, I hold a stock minimum for 1 year because as per Indian law, after one year holding, returns are tax-free so some of my stock runs more than 15% in this 1-year holding period, for example,. I recommended and bought Pricol Ltd. at 16.35 in August 2013 and in July 2014 CMP of Pricol Ltd. is 46.65 and stock already gave 185.23% profit to me in July 2014, but I did not sell it because my 1 year is not yet complete. After August 2014 when my minimum holding period is over for this stock, I sell out this stock at 55.30 and get 238.22% tax-free profits, one other great point to remember if stock price crossed its net sell per share per year and traded 20% above base price then it is wise to book profits.

Overall, there is not any sure rule for the exit, it all depends on greed and your experience in the share market.

How do we decide which exit strategy to follow?

In this book, I give these three exit strategies:

- Target price of 15% profits from the entry price
- 20% + of Base price
- Predicted target price TP = (NSPY + Book Value + Base Price)/3), where NSPY stands for Net Selling per Year (per share) Predicted target price TP = (NSPY + Book value

+ Base Price)/3 is best, but personally I did not follow this after my holding of 1 year if my profit is above 15%. I book my profit because I rotate my money and booking profits always protected us from downfalls.

Summary

1. If stock price goes up with volumes and market conditions are favourable for your stock, then hold it.
2. There is not any sure rule for the exit, it all depends on greed and your experience in the share market.

❐

26
How to Recover Your Loss in Stock Market

It is possible that you buy this book too late and your portfolio is in loss.

Now I tell you a sure formula to recover your portfolio loss.

Check 200 DMA of your stock. If your loss-making stock is traded 5% or more below its 200 DMA and stock crosses this 200 DMA from upper price to lower price, then sell it at any market price and book your loss.

For example, you invest in Stock A @105 per share, when you invest 200, DMA of Stock A is 98; after few days, your stock falls from 105 to 92, this means your stock fell 5% or more below its 200 DMA and stock crosses this 200 DMA from upper price(105) to lower price (92). This is a sign of fresh weakness, and stock price may fall more, so sell your stock when you are trapped in this type of situation.

Now watch 200 DMA of your stock per day. You can calculate 200 DMA by yourself and find it on moneycontrol site, watch my YouTube video about this:

https://www.youtube.com/watch?v=rSVbuSddVBU

When your stock crosses this 200 DMA from low price to higher price, then buy it again if you already sell this or if you miss-selling and still hold in loss then invest double amount average out at this level and invest the double amount in same stock.

For example, when your stock crosses its 200 DMA 98 in downside, then DMA is also falling as stock falls and if you sell it near 90-93, then it will be possible that stock falls near 50-60 in the next 3-6 months. In this situation, DMA will also fall near 67-72 so when stock crosses this 200 DMA upside, then buy it again if you have already bought it.

If you do not sell near 90-93 in a downtrend and hold this loss-making stock which you buy @105 then, this time, invest the double amount to average out when the stock crosses its 200 DMA in an uptrend, and you wonder in 80% + cases, you recover your loss within 30 days. Watch my YouTube video for more detail.

In YouTube, search box-type 'Mahesh Kaushik How To Recover Loss,' You will find the video link.

Summary

If you read this book completely, and now I think you may understand that investing in the stock market is the world's simplest business, but people lose their money because they don't treat their business as a business. They speculate on the market and try to make some easy money. So if you apply concepts of this book to your investing and work hard at choosing a good stock in my theory, then you may always win in the stock market. Tell me how much you like this book. Please send your comments to me at mahesh2073@yahoo.com

My main motto for writing this book is to make you self-dependent so that you will choose good stocks with the help of research terms given in this book. But if you still find it difficult to choose a stock for investment, then please feel free to download my free app 'Multibagger Stocks Sharegenius' from Google play store.

In this app, I have published full research reports of stocks that fulfil terms given in the book and also provided stocks that break out over their 30, 50, 150 and 200 DMA.

I spent 12 precious years in writing this book; if you do not understand any of the terms given in the book, then please do not put a negative review because followers' negative review may break my heart. So, before putting a negative review, please feel free to email your concern to me. I will try to resolve your problem, and if you are still unsatisfied, then you will be free to put your negative comment.

My email address is: mahesh2073@yahoo.com

Due to 25,000 followers, I am unable to attend your phone calls and reply all e-mails; so, please be patient and forward your e-mail again if you did not get any reply within seven days.

Here is a summary of this book, if you remember and follow these points, then you will find that the stock market business is the world's simplest business because in the stock market business, you start your business with very small capital. Even if in $100, you start your stock market business with buying one company stock or buying some units of mutual fund. So, please remember these golden points again for stock market investing.

1. Treat your stock market business like a retail shop and keep many varieties of stocks in your portfolio.
2. Always buy a good dividend paying stock.
3. Always buy new stocks in market fall when good stocks are traded at a discount.
4. Never average out a non-performing stock.
5. Sell your stocks when a stock gives you 15% + return and rotate your money. Not to be emotionally attached to any company, because the shopkeeper doesn't hold his shop

item when the buyer gives profit to shopkeeper, then he/she will not hesitate to sell shop item.

6. Always start your buying from a low price stock which is fundamentally good. For example, download price list of all the stocks in Microsoft Excel format and then sort out this list with stock close price smallest to the largest pattern. Then check the smallest close price stock fundamentals. If it fulfils your criteria, then buy a minimum lot of it and if not, then check next stock, repeat this process and build your share market retail shop.
7. Decide a minimum investment amount in a particular stock, for example, if you have 50,000 dollars then you will decide $100 for investing in a company and buy 500 good dividend-paying company with your research.
8. Do not buy more than one company in a trading week because it will give you time to research on fundamentals of companies and give you a chance of buying at a lower price.
9. Always buy a stock below 20% of its three years' average price (which I called base price) and try to book profits above 20% of the base price.
10. When your trade gives you 15% profits than holding it with trailing stop-loss, 15% is a minimum range of profits, but it does not mean that you sell your stocks at a trigger price of 15%. After 15%, watch your stock closely.
11. If the stock price goes up with volumes and market conditions are favourable for your stock, then hold it.
12. There is no sure rule for an exit-out, it all depends on your greed and your experience in the share market.

13. Do not see net profits of a company always; see net revenue or net sale of the company.
14. Choose stocks which have higher net revenue per share. My new term for this is NSPS (Net sell per share).
15. Buy when the market price of a stock is 20% below its one-year net revenue per share. And sell when stock current market price crosses one-year net revenue per share.
16. Decide your fundamental target for a sell-out stock-for this purpose average out net revenue per share, book value and the base price of stock, then reducing it 10%, this is the fundamental target of stock.
17. Buy below 15% of fundamental target for making profits because we sell our stocks when stock price crosses fundamental target price.
18. If the stock traded 20% or more above its fundamental target, then avoid it because the valuation of the stock is high and it may be available at a lower price in market fall.
19. Do not buy a huge holding in your fancy stock.
20. If any stock is your fancy, then make a long-term equity SIP in particular stock.
21. When you hold a huge quantity of any stock in profits, then do not book profit in all of your holdings.
22. Divide all of your holdings in 1/10 parts and if this stock starts fallings then sell 1/10 part at every 30% price fall.
23. Choose your initial investment amount in each stock.
24. Book your profit when the stock is rising more than 15% and rotate your money in new stock.
25. Every time, increase 7.5% in your new investment amount.

26. Big traders make a speculation of pricing in stock markets. So try to identify the speculation through bulk deals' history.
27. Avoid a stock which has a recent bulk (block) deal. When bulk deals happen in any stock, trading near its year-high and all-time higher, then the downturn in this stock may be starting in the coming 1-2 months.
28. Stock below face value is risky so always check other fundamental points like base price, one-year net revenue per share, recent bulk deals, recent stock splits and bonus before you buy stocks below the face value.
29. When you compare prices of the two stocks, then always see their face value for identifying which stock is cheap.
30. Do not buy if a stock falls more than 50% from year-high. And in opposite, do not buy if a stock rises more than 100% from year-high.
31. When you are trapped in a loss-making investment, then track its year-high year-low ratio. When stock crash is more than 50% from year-high, it means year-high or year low ratio is more than 2; so this is a sign of long-term bearish trend, then it is time to sell. After some years, when year-high or year-low ratio is less than 1.5, this time, you will buy your same quantity again.
32. Always avoid a stock in which promoters hold below 15% or promoters reduce their holdings in the last 1 year.
33. Avoid a stock which traded 20% above its base price.
34. Choose a stock which traded below its one-year net revenue per share.

35. Avoid a stock which has a recent bulk deal in the last 2 years.
36. Avoid a stock which has a recent stock split and bonus in the last 2 years because after a bonus issue and split in the face value, the number of stocks is rising, so company net EPS is diluted after the bonus.
37. Do not trade in future and option and intraday speculation. Do not average out at every fall.
38. Do not borrow money for stock market investing.
39. If the last close price – last open price = negative figure and last close price – today open price is also a negative figure, then you may make short positions because the stock is bearish.
40. If the last close price – last open price = positive figure and last close price – today open price is also a positive figure, then you may make long positions because the stock is bullish.
41. The stock market index is not a fair criterion for investing because stocks in a market index are changed from time to time. Always see particular share price movement, not to consider index movement.
42. In mutual fund investing, invest only in SIP method. Do not forget to book profit in mutual fund SIP; it will secure your realized profit from any market fall; also balance your portfolio in debt, and equity mutual fund investment is a passive investment.
43. Choose the dividend option in ELSS.
44. Penny stocks may give you multiple returns. If you choose a good penny stock, invest only 10% of your total investment amount in penny stocks because they are risky.
45. It is necessary for a small investor to keep some

knowledge of technical analysis and before making an investment, it is advisable to check moving averages, RSI, support, and resistance to making a good decision but always invest on the basis of fundamentals.

46. It is believed that if a trader keeps Dalbergia Sissoo tree bark in his pocket, then he will be lucky in trading.
47. Do not blindly follow every analyst on TV, apply your own common sense before investing.
48. Try to understand the differences of a short-term technical tip and long-term fundamental investing.
49. Swapping from a loss-making stock to another stock is not a good policy.
50. Future and options trading is not for small investors; it is a tool for big institutional investors and speculators.
51. If you invest initially $100 and add $10 per month and your money is growing 84% annually, then after 20 years, you have nearly $7,18,03,722.

Download my Multibagger Stocks Sharegenius app from Google play store. It is free of cost, with the help of this app, you get all of my future recommendations and discuss your problems with me.

Regards

Mahesh Chander Kaushik

Disclaimer

Trading in the stock market is very risky. Please analyse for yourself what your risk profile is. This book is not perfect. This is not an advisory book to buy or sell advice. The contents of 'this book's only for educational purposes. No liability is accepted for any content in 'The Winning Theory in Stock Market' book. This book is subject to Pindwara (India) jurisdiction only. The author is a registered research analyst with SEBI. His comments are an expression of opinion only and should not be construed in any manner whatsoever as recommendations to buy or sell a stock, option, future, bond, commodity, index or any other financial instrument at any time. While he believes his statements to be true, they always depend on the reliability of his credible sources. The author recommends that you consult with a qualified investment advisor, one licensed by appropriate regulatory agencies in your legal jurisdiction, before making any investment decisions, and that you confirm the facts on your own before making important investment commitments.

—Mahesh Chander Kaushik
TRA *Tehsil* Office Pindwara
India– 307 022
mahesh2073@yahoo.com

Appendix

List of 171 changes in Nifty

Event Date	Scrip Name	Description
18-09-1996	ABB India Ltd.	Inclusion into Index
18-09-1996	Asian Paints Ltd.	Inclusion into Index
18-09-1996	East India Hotels Ltd.	Inclusion into Index
18-09-1996	Glaxo (India) Ltd.	Inclusion into Index
18-09-1996	Mahindra & Mahindra Ltd.	Inclusion into Index
18-09-1996	Nestle India Limited	Inclusion into Index
18-09-1996	Chambal Fertilizers & Chemicals Ltd.	Exclusion from Index
18-09-1996	Hero Honda Motors Ltd.	Exclusion from Index
18-09-1996	Apollo Tyres Ltd.	Exclusion from Index
18-09-1996	Indian Aluminium Co. Ltd.	Exclusion from Index
18-09-1996	Madras Refineries Ltd.	Exclusion from Index
18-09-1996	Nagarjuna Fertilizers & Chemicals Ltd.	Exclusion from Index
07-05-1997	Mahanagar Telephone Nigam Ltd.	Inclusion into Index

07-05-1997	Brooke Bond Lipton India Ltd.	Exclusion from Index
14-05-1997	Bharat Heavy Electricals Ltd.	Inclusion into Index
14-05-1997	Hindustan Petroleum Corporation Ltd.	Inclusion into Index
14-05-1997	SCICI Ltd.	Exclusion from Index
14-05-1997	Dr. Reddy's Laboratories Ltd.	Exclusion from Index
24-12-1997	Bharat Petroleum Corporation Ltd.	Inclusion into Index
24-12-1997	Essar Gujarat Ltd.	Exclusion from Index
07-10-1998	Bank of India	Inclusion into Index
07-10-1998	Cipla Ltd.	Inclusion into Index
07-10-1998	Hero Honda Motors Ltd.	Inclusion into Index
07-10-1998	Infosys Technologies Ltd.	Inclusion into Index
07-10-1998	NIIT Ltd.	Inclusion into Index
07-10-1998	Procter & Gamble India Ltd.	Inclusion into Index
07-10-1998	SmithKline Beecham Consumer Healthcare Ltd.	Inclusion into Index
07-10-1998	Thermax Ltd.	Exclusion from Index
07-10-1998	Andhra Valley Power Supply Co. Ltd.	Exclusion from Index

07-10-1998	Ashok Leyland Ltd.	Exclusion from Index
07-10-1998	Bharat Petroleum Corporation Ltd.	Exclusion from Index
07-10-1998	Indo Gulf Corporation Ltd.	Exclusion from Index
07-10-1998	Mangalore Refinery & Petrochemicals Ltd.	Exclusion from Index
07-10-1998	Ponds (India) Ltd.	Exclusion from Index
26-05-1999	Dr. Reddy's Laboratories Ltd.	Inclusion into Index
26-05-1999	Novartis India Ltd.	Inclusion into Index
26-05-1999	Reckitt & Colman India Ltd.	Inclusion into Index
26-05-1999	Arvind Mills Ltd.	Exclusion from Index
26-05-1999	Great Eastern Shipping Company Ltd.	Exclusion from Index
26-05-1999	Reliance Capital Ltd.	Exclusion from Index
08-09-1999	Britannia Industries Ltd.	Inclusion into Index
08-09-1999	Satyam Computer Services Ltd.	Inclusion into Index
08-09-1999	Industrial Finance Corporation Of India Ltd.	Exclusion from Index
08-09-1999	Indian Rayon & Industries Ltd.	Exclusion from Index

10-05-2000	Dabur India Ltd.	Inclusion into Index
10-05-2000	TVS Suzuki Ltd.	Exclusion from Index
24-05-2000	HCL Infosystems Ltd.	Inclusion into Index
24-05-2000	Zee Telefilms Ltd.	Inclusion into Index
24-05-2000	EIH Ltd.	Exclusion from Index
24-05-2000	Industrial Development Bank of India Ltd.	Exclusion from Index
01-09-2000	Digital Equipment (India) Ltd.	Inclusion into Index
01-09-2000	Bank of India	Exclusion from Index
17-01-2002	Sun Pharmaceutical Industries Ltd.	Inclusion into Index
17-01-2002	Wipro Ltd.	Inclusion into Index
17-01-2002	HCL Infosystems Ltd.	Exclusion from Index
17-01-2002	Kochi Refineries Ltd.	Exclusion from Index
25-01-2002	ICICI Bank Ltd.	Inclusion into Index
25-01-2002	Reckitt Benckiser (India) Ltd.	Exclusion from Index
31-05-2002	Videsh Sanchar Nigam Ltd.	Inclusion into Index
31-05-2002	ICICI Ltd.	Exclusion from Index
10-10-2002	Shipping Corporation of India Ltd.	Inclusion into Index

10-10-2002	Reliance Petroleum Ltd.	Exclusion from Index
28-10-2002	Bharat Petroleum Corporation Ltd.	Inclusion into Index
28-10-2002	HCL Technologies Ltd.	Inclusion into Index
28-10-2002	Procter & Gamble India Ltd.	Exclusion from Index
28-10-2002	Asian Paints Ltd.	Exclusion from Index
02-05-2003	Gas Authority of India Ltd.	Inclusion into Index
02-05-2003	National Aluminium Co. Ltd.	Inclusion into Index
02-05-2003	Novartis India Ltd.	Exclusion from Index
02-05-2003	Castrol (India) Ltd.	Exclusion from Index
04-08-2003	Steel Authority of India Ltd.	Inclusion into Index
04-08-2003	Nestle India Limited	Exclusion from Index
01-03-2004	Bharti Tele-Ventures Ltd.	Inclusion into Index
01-03-2004	Maruti Udyog Limited	Inclusion into Index
01-03-2004	Glaxo Smithkline Consumer Healthcare Ltd.	Exclusion from Index
01-03-2004	NIIT Ltd.	Exclusion from Index

12-04-2004	Oil & Natural Gas Corporation Ltd.	Inclusion into Index
12-04-2004	Digital Globalsoft Ltd.	Exclusion from Index
24-05-2004	Punjab National Bank	Inclusion into Index
24-05-2004	Larsen & Toubro Ltd.	Exclusion from Index
10-12-2004	Larsen & Toubro Ltd.	Inclusion into Index
10-12-2004	Britannia Industries Ltd.	Exclusion from Index
25-02-2005	Tata Consultancy Services Ltd.	Inclusion into Index
25-02-2005	Indian Hotels Co. Ltd.	Exclusion from Index
26-09-2005	Jet Airways (India) Ltd.	Inclusion into Index
26-09-2005	Colgate Palmolive (India) Ltd.	Exclusion from Index
27-06-2006	Suzlon Energy Ltd.	Inclusion into Index
27-06-2006	Siemens Ltd.	Inclusion into Index
27-06-2006	Shipping Corporation of India Ltd.	Exclusion from Index
27-06-2006	Tata Chemicals Ltd.	Exclusion from Index
01-09-2006	Reliance Communications Ltd.	Inclusion into Index
01-09-2006	Tata Tea Limited	Exclusion from Index
04-04-2007	Reliance Petroleum Ltd.	Inclusion into Index
04-04-2007	Sterlite Industries (India) Ltd.	Inclusion into Index

04-04-2007	Jet Airways (India) Ltd.	Exclusion from Index
04-04-2007	Oriental Bank of Commerce	Exclusion from Index
24-09-2007	NTPC Ltd.	Inclusion into Index
24-09-2007	Dabur India Ltd.	Exclusion from Index
05-10-2007	Unitech Ltd.	Inclusion into Index
05-10-2007	Indian Petrochemicals Corporation Ltd.	Exclusion from Index
12-12-2007	Idea Cellular Ltd.	Inclusion into Index
12-12-2007	Cairn India Ltd.	Inclusion into Index
12-12-2007	Mahanagar Telephone Nigam Ltd.	Exclusion from Index
12-12-2007	Hindustan Petroleum Corporation Ltd.	Exclusion from Index
14-03-2008	DLF Ltd.	Inclusion into Index
14-03-2008	Power Grid Corporation of India Ltd.	Inclusion into Index
14-03-2008	Glaxo Smithkline Pharmaceuticals Ltd.	Exclusion from Index
14-03-2008	Bajaj Auto Ltd.	Exclusion from Index
10-09-2008	Reliance Power Ltd.	Inclusion into Index
10-09-2008	Dr. Reddy's Laboratories Ltd.	Exclusion from Index
12-01-2009	Reliance Capital Ltd.	Inclusion into Index
12-01-2009	Satyam Computer Services Ltd.	Exclusion from Index
27-03-2009	Axis Bank Ltd.	Inclusion into Index

27-03-2009	Zee Entertainment Enterprises Ltd.	Exclusion from Index
17-06-2009	Jindal Steel & Power Ltd.	Inclusion into Index
17-06-2009	Reliance Petroleum Ltd.	Exclusion from Index
22-10-2009	Jaiprakash Associates Ltd.	Inclusion into Index
22-10-2009	Infrastructure Development Finance Company Limited	Inclusion into Index
22-10-2009	Tata Communications Ltd.	Exclusion from Index
22-10-2009	National Aluminium Co. Ltd.	Exclusion from Index
08-04-2010	Kotak Mahindra Bank Ltd.	Inclusion into Index
08-04-2010	Grasim Industries Ltd.	Exclusion from Index
01-10-2010	Sesa Goa Limited	
01-10-2010	Dr. Reddy's Laboratories Ltd.	Inclusion into Index
01-10-2010	Bajaj Auto Ltd.	Inclusion into Index
01-10-2010	Unitech Ltd.	Exclusion from Index
01-10-2010	Idea Cellular Ltd.	Exclusion from Index
01-10-2010	ABB India Ltd.	Exclusion from Index
25-03-2011	Grasim Industries Ltd.	Inclusion into Index

25-03-2011	Suzlon Energy Ltd.	Exclusion from Index
10-10-2011	Coal India Ltd.	Inclusion into Index
10-10-2011	Reliance Capital Ltd.	Exclusion from Index
27-04-2012	Asian Paints Ltd.	Inclusion into Index
27-04-2012	Bank of Baroda	Inclusion into Index
27-04-2012	Reliance Communications Ltd.	Exclusion from Index
27-04-2012	Reliance Power Ltd.	Exclusion from Index
28-09-2012	Lupin Ltd.	Inclusion into Index
28-09-2012	UltraTech Cement Ltd.	Inclusion into Index
28-09-2012	Steel Authority of India Ltd.	Exclusion from Index
28-09-2012	Sterlite Industries (India) Ltd.	Exclusion from Index
01-04-2013	IndusInd Bank Ltd.	Inclusion into Index
01-04-2013	NMDC Ltd.	Inclusion into Index
01-04-2013	Siemens Ltd.	Exclusion from Index
01-04-2013	Wipro Ltd.	Exclusion from Index
27-09-2013	Wipro Ltd.	Inclusion into Index
27-09-2013	Reliance Infrastructure Ltd.	Exclusion from Index
28-03-2014	Jaiprakash Associates Ltd.	Exclusion from Index
28-03-2014	Ranbaxy Laboratories Ltd.	Exclusion from Index

28-03-2014	Tech Mahindra Ltd.	Inclusion into Index
28-03-2014	United Spirits Ltd.	Inclusion into Index
19-09-2014	United Spirits Ltd.	Exclusion from Index
19-09-2014	Zee Entertainment Enterprises Ltd.	Inclusion into Index
27-03-2015	DLF Ltd.	Exclusion from Index
27-03-2015	Jindal Steel & Power Ltd.	Exclusion from Index
27-03-2015	Idea Cellular Ltd.	Inclusion into Index
27-03-2015	Yes Bank Ltd.	Inclusion into Index
29-05-2015	IDFC Ltd	Exclusion from Index
29-05-2015	Bosch Ltd.	Inclusion into Index
28-09-2015	NMDC Ltd.	Exclusion from Index
28-09-2015	Adani Ports & Special Economic Zone Ltd.	Inclusion into Index
04-01-2016	Cairn India Ltd.	Exclusion from Index
04-01-2016	Punjab National Bank	Exclusion from Index
04-01-2016	Vedanta Ltd.	Exclusion from Index
04-01-2016	Aurobindo Pharma Ltd.	Inclusion into Index
04-01-2016	Bharti Infratel Ltd.	Inclusion into Index
04-01-2016	Eicher Motors Ltd.	Inclusion into Index
04-01-2016	Tata Motors Ltd. DVR	Inclusion into Index

03-31-2017	Bharat Heavy Electricals Ltd.	Exclusion from Index
03-31-2017	Idea Cellular Ltd.	Exclusion from Index
03-31-2017	Indiabulls Housing Finance Ltd.	Inclusion into Index
03-31-2017	Indian Oil Corporation Ltd.	Inclusion into Index

❑❑❑